Disney · PIXAR
INSIDE OUT

Read-Along
STORYBOOK AND CD

This is the story of Riley and her Emotions.
You can read along with me in your book.
You will know it is time to turn the page
when you hear this sound. . . .
Let's begin now.

Printed in the United States of America
First Edition, May 2015   10 9 8 7 6 5 4 3 2 1
Library of Congress Control Number: 2014954387
V381-8386-5-15079
ISBN 978-1-4847-1279-5

For more Disney Press fun, visit www.disneybooks.com

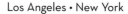

Disney PRESS

Los Angeles • New York

SUSTAINABLE FORESTRY INITIATIVE
Certified Chain of Custody
At Least 20% Certified Forest Content
www.sfiprogram.org
SFI-00993
For Text Only

When baby Riley opened her eyes for the first time, Joy was there.

Joy was an Emotion that lived inside Riley's mind. She worked at Headquarters, where it was her job to help Riley feel happy.

Joy watched as Riley's parents gazed at their new daughter. "Aren't you a little bundle of joy."

Riley's happy memories were saved in golden spheres, and Joy made sure she had lots of them. Joy loved Riley. **"Just Riley and me. Forever . . ."**

But she wasn't alone with Riley for long. Thirty-three seconds after Riley was born, another Emotion showed up . . . and she was very different from Joy.

"I'm **Sadness**."

Joy didn't like the sound of that! "Can I just . . . If you could . . . I just want to fix that. Thanks." Joy stopped Sadness from using Riley's Headquarters console as often as possible.

Soon more Emotions arrived at Headquarters, and each one had a different job.

Fear was in charge of safety. **"Ahhh! Look out! No!"**

If Riley encountered something dangerous, like a loose power cord or a big dog, he took control. "Easy, easy . . . ahhh . . . Oh, we're good. We're good."

Disgust's good taste kept Riley from being poisoned. "That is not brightly colored or shaped like a dinosaur. Hold on, guys . . . It's **broccoli**!"

Anger stepped in whenever things were unfair. "Wait. Did he just say we couldn't have dessert? *Grrraaaahh!*"

And Sadness made Riley . . . **sad**. Joy understood why the others were important, but why did Riley need Sadness?

Riley's memories were all saved in different-colored spheres, each matching an Emotion. Joy was proud that most of the memories were golden. "Another perfect day!" But when Riley's family moved from Minnesota to San Francisco, everything changed.

Riley didn't like moving. She missed all her friends.

Inside Headquarters, Sadness kept touching happy memories of Riley's old home and turning them blue! "Something's wrong with me. It's like I'm having a breakdown."

Joy tried to keep Sadness out of the way. "This is the **circle of Sadness**. Your job is to make sure that all the sadness stays inside of it."

On her first day at her new school, Riley introduced herself in class. **"Everything's different now. Since we moved . . ."** While thinking about her old home, Riley started crying in front of everyone!

Then, for the first time ever, a *blue* core memory was formed! Core memories powered Riley's personality by creating islands in her mind devoted to her favorite things, like Honesty Island and Goofball Island. The Islands of Personality made her who she was. Riley's original five core memories were all a joyful yellow.

Joy wanted to get rid of the blue memory, so she tried to send it away through a memory flush vacuum tube—but Sadness protected it. **"That's a core memory!"**

As they struggled, they knocked the other core memories out of their holder. With all the core memories disconnected, the personality islands went dark. "Ahh!"

Then the powerful vacuum tube sucked up Joy, Sadness, and the core memories, blasting them toward the Memory Dump.

But on the way, the tube cracked open. Joy and Sadness fell to the ground. "Waaaaah-oof!"

Joy looked at the lifeless islands in the distance and knew she had to return the core memories to Headquarters. "I'm coming, Riley." If she made it across the bridge to Goofball Island, she could walk back to Headquarters.

But without any core memories in place, **Goofball Island began to fall apart**!

Joy and Sadness would need to find a new way to get back to Headquarters. The two walked toward Long Term Memory, where they ran into someone Joy hadn't seen in years. "I know you. You're **Bing Bong**! Riley's imaginary friend!"

Riley used to pretend to travel everywhere with Bing Bong in his rocket. Now Bing Bong was looking through Long Term Memory for something special. "I thought maybe if I could find a really good memory, Riley would remember me. And then I'll be a part of Riley's life again!"

Joy asked Bing Bong if he knew how to get back to Headquarters. **"Just take the Train of Thought!"**

On the way to the train station, he gave them a tour of Imagination Land. It was amazing! They even discovered a new area: Imaginary Boyfriend.

Then Bing Bong noticed parts of Preschool World being torn down to make room for Riley's new interests.

He spotted his rocket being thrown away. "No, you can't take my rocket to the dump!" But it was too late. Bing Bong began to cry big candy tears.

Sadness sat down. **"I'm sorry they took your rocket. They took something that you loved. It's gone . . . forever."** Talking to Sadness helped Bing Bong stop crying, but Joy couldn't understand why. How had Sadness made Bing Bong feel better?

"C'mon. The train station is this way."

But the train soon stopped for the night. Riley had fallen asleep!

Hoping they could wake her up, they headed to **Dream Productions**, where Riley's dreams were made.

Bing Bong held the memories while Joy and Sadness ran in front of the dream camera sharing a dog costume. They tried to make Riley so happy she would wake up laughing. "Woo! Let's party!"

The Dream Director was not happy. She called security.

Bing Bong was taken to the Subconscious, where Riley's darkest fears lived. There, he was trapped by Jangles the Clown!

While Joy and Sadness rescued Bing Bong, seeing the spooky clown gave Joy an idea. Jangles could scare Riley awake! "H-hello. D-did you know that it was time for a ba-bah-birthday party?"

"Did you say 'birthday'?" Jangles chased them onto the Dream Productions set and terrified everyone!

The scary dream woke Riley and **the train started moving**. Joy, Sadness, and Bing Bong happily hopped on.

Back at Headquarters, the other Emotions were scrambling, trying to figure out what to do.

Anger thought Riley should run away. "All the good core memories were made in Minnesota. Ergo, we go back to Minnesota and make more. **Who's with me?**"

Disgust agreed. **"Yeah, let's do it."**

The Emotions made Riley steal her mom's credit card and pack a bag for Minnesota.

On the train, Sadness and Joy discussed their favorite memory. They both loved the day Riley's hockey team and parents had shown up to cheer for her after a hard day. But Sadness liked the sad part. "It was the day the Prairie Dogs lost the big play-off game. Riley missed the winning shot. She felt awful. She wanted to quit."

Joy didn't understand her. Why like the sad stuff?

Then Honesty Island started to break apart, causing the train to skid off the tracks. **They leaped from the train** just before it plunged into the Memory Dump far below!

They ran toward a bridge to the last standing island: Family Island. But as Riley left her house for the bus, Family Island began to fall, taking the bridge along with it.

As the world around them crumbled, **Joy and Bing Bong fell into the Memory Dump**. **"Ahhhhhh!"**

"Joy!" Sadness stood alone on a cliff, hopelessly looking down. If they couldn't escape from the dump, Joy and Bing Bong would fade away and be forgotten.

For the first time, Joy felt like giving up. She looked at Riley's memories, remembering the good times. She watched the one that she and Sadness liked.

"Mom and Dad . . . the team . . . they came to help because of Sadness." **Joy finally understood how important Sadness was.** By not letting Riley feel sad, Joy was keeping her from feeling happy, too. "We have to get back up there!"

Joy had an idea. They could use Bing Bong's trashed rocket to fly themselves out of the dump!

They tried and tried, but each time, the rocket fell short. Together, two of them were too heavy. **Bing Bong knew what he had to do.**

Without Joy noticing, Bing Bong hopped out of the rocket. It worked! "Woo-hooo! Bing Bong, we did it! We—Bing Bong?"

Bing Bong looked up at Joy, laughing and dancing. "You made it! Ha-ha! Go! Go save Riley!" He waved good-bye as he disappeared.

Joy raced off to find Sadness, but Sadness hopped onto a cloud and flew away. **"I only make everything worse."** Sadness thought Riley would be better off without her.

"Come back!" Using the Imaginary Boyfriend Generator, Joy created a tower of boyfriends and stood on top. *"Now!"* The boyfriends launched her onto a trampoline, and she bounced up, catching Sadness in the air! "Gotcha!"

Joy and Sadness kept flying toward Headquarters and landed against the window.

The other Emotions tried to let them in, but the window wouldn't open!

Disgust had an idea. She made fun of Anger until he got so mad his head was on fire. ***"Daaaaaahhh!"*** Then she grabbed Anger and used the heat to cut a hole in the glass!

Finally, Joy and Sadness climbed through.

Riley had just stepped onto the bus, on her way to Minnesota.

Joy knew what to do. "Sadness, it's up to you."

"Me? I can't, Joy."

"Yes, you can. Riley needs *you*."

"Okay."

With Sadness in control, Riley stood up. **"Wait! Stop! I wanna get off."** She got off the bus and ran home.

Sadness continued to help as Riley talked to her parents. "I know you don't want me to, but . . . I miss home. I miss Minnesota." Letting Riley finally express her sadness was the only way she would feel better again.

Her parents understood. "We're not mad. You know what? I miss Minnesota, too."

As the family hugged, Joy and Sadness smiled at each other. They knew now that the best way to help Riley was side by side. From now on, all the Emotions would **work together as a team**.